Shivers

Jane Ferguson

Hippo Books
Scholastic Publications Ltd.,
London

Contents

Scholastic Publications Ltd.,
10 Earlham Street, London WC2H 9LN, UK

Scholastic Inc.,
730 Broadway, New York, NY 10003, USA

Scholastic Tab Publications Ltd.,
123 Newkirk Road, Richmond Hill,
Ontario L4C 3G5, Canada

Ashton Scholastic Pty. Ltd.,
PO Box 579, Gosford, New South Wales,
Australia

Ashton Scholastic Ltd.,
165 Marua Road, Panmure, Auckland 6,
New Zealand

First published by Scholastic Publications Ltd; 1985
Reprinted 1986, 1987

Text copyright © Jane Ferguson, 1985
Illustration copyright © Terry McKenna

ISBN 0 590 70311 0

All rights reserved
Printed by Cox & Wyman Ltd., Reading, Berks.
Typeset in Baskerville by Gilbert Composing Services,
Leighton Buzzard, Bedfordshire

Have you ever had that creeping cold, numbing feeling that starts at the base of your skull, puts the brain into shock, and sends chilling waves surging up and down your spine? It's the feeling you'll get when you read *Shivers*! Ginger, who gets trapped in the basement of a big department store with the window dummies; Cathy, who watches a terrifying drama being acted out in the pictures on her bedroom wall; and Uncle Charlie's anything-but-harmless leopardskin rug are just three of the spooky stories in this collection for readers of ten to twelve.

Kevin's Story:

Spectacles in the Abbey

"OK, OK, I'm coming!"

Just one picture, that was all. Before the abbey closed and the last few visitors, like Kevin and his parents, were turned out.

They had been late getting there in the first place, and Kevin hadn't wanted to come in. It was Mum, funnily enough, who was dead keen on castles and old ruins. She had dragged him in, and now she was nagging him to get out. Mum always worried about doing the right thing. Perhaps she was scared of being shut inside an old ruin like this at night. Kevin grinned. That would serve her right! She might not be so keen after that. Anyway, now he was here, he just wanted to get this one shot.

He had been told often enough about having the light behind you when you took pictures, but he liked the way the evening sun was slanting through that arch. He was sure his brilliant new camera would make a great picture out of it. Dad had said it was a new doorway, built halfway along the original long aisle and not really part of the old abbey. But, even so, it was still over three hundred years old.

Kevin was standing where the monks—long, long before that doorway had been given its new door—used to come downstairs in the middle of the night for prayers. Kevin didn't think he'd have liked that much, especially in winter. Bet they would have been grumpy.

Behind him, through the old arches, used to be the busiest, liveliest parts of the abbey. Now they were covered in smooth, well-cut grass, soft and quiet, with just the stony outlines of the old rooms pushing through. Soft and quiet and dead. Like the men who had once lived here.

"Kev! What on earth are you *doing?*" It was his Mum calling again.

If he could somehow get high up he'd be able to fit more of the arch into his picture. What was that big stone slab—a tomb? Or perhaps an altar? Well, it wasn't anything now. He took off his glasses and laid them on the stone while he climbed on to it. They were always a nuisance when he was taking pictures. Yes, that was better! Through the arch the sun had almost set behind the hills and it looked really terrific.

He had just taken a shot of it when an angry shout made him jump and look round guiltily. He couldn't see anyone, but he knew he was being ticked off. He scrambled down quickly from the slab, mumbling a sort of apology to the air. He'd got to go anyway, the light was getting far too dim for photographs. He ran to join Mum and Dad. They were chatting to the curator in the little ticket office who was waiting to lock up.

"You'll never get a picture in this light," said his Dad. Kevin said he wouldn't know if he didn't *try*, would he, and his Mum said he didn't seem to realise how much films cost, and he needn't expect her to help out . . . Kevin had heard it all before and stopped listening.

They crossed the road to the car park, empty now except for their own car. Probably nothing much happened in the evenings in such a small town. As they opened up the car they waved to the abbey curator who had now shut his office and was climbing on his motorbike. He waved back as he rode off down the road.

Kevin had been sitting in the car for only a few moments when he suddenly realised something awful.

"My glasses! I've left them in the abbey! I took them off to take a picture and I must have . . . Oh *no!*" and his voice trailed away in misery.

He thought his Mum would explode, but she must have thought he was upset enough already. She simply put on her let's-keep-calm voice. The curator might live nearby, she said, and they could ask to get back in.

They all got out of the car again, and walked up the hill to the little High Street. Dad asked in the bar of a hotel, and Mum asked in the small library. Everyone was willing to help, but no one knew where the curator lived.

Wretchedly, they walked back down the hill. They stood looking over the railings at the ruins as if they thought they could conjure up the glasses by wishing.

At last Dad said, "Well, no one's going to steal them, are they? So let's just come back tomorrow morning."

Kevin groaned. What a waste of time when there were only two days of the holiday left. There must be some other way. After all, he knew exactly where he'd left them.

"Let me climb over—I'm sure I could."

His mum looked horrified, but his Dad seemed to think it was quite an idea.

They examined the railings together. All

round the abbey grounds was a low wall, with railings fixed on top. On one side of the gate, by the cemetery, they were tall and spiked, but on the other side they were shorter and topped by a smooth bar.

"Easy!" yelled Kevin, loud with sheer relief.

"O.K., but let's make sure you can get back out, Kev, 'cos we won't be there to heave you up," said Dad.

They found a spot with a bank on the other side of the wall, where Kevin could climb over easily by himself. His parents promised to stay marking the place till he came back. It felt peculiar to be doing something really wrong, like climbing railings, with them cheering him on.

"Right, I'll just go and look for my glasses," he announced in an awkward, extra-loud voice, in case anyone was watching them. But there was no one else there at all.

Kevin walked back through the ruins, now shadowy in the evening light. He went under the arch where, half-an-hour ago, he had photographed the sunset, and saw at the end of the aisle the great stone slab he had climbed on.

He ran up to it, and then stopped. He was sure he had put his glasses down there! But he couldn't see them. Trouble was, when you lost your glasses, you couldn't see *anything* very well. He walked round the slab, and looked anxiously at the ground.

Knowing he was being silly (after all, he wasn't *blind* without glasses!), he patted the slab all over with his hand. Then he heard a muffled shout behind him.

Not again! He turned round to explain this time, and saw, standing against the wall, a figure dressed in something black and pointing at him angrily. He couldn't see him at all clearly—surely, he thought, it wasn't as dark as this a moment ago?

But it was growing dark very quickly now. Kevin felt shut in by darkness, as if the sky were no longer above him. He felt as if the night had closed round him, like the walls of a building. He turned back, holding tight to the edge of the slab, and saw in front of him a great crowd of figures beginning to take shape in the gloom.

As he watched them, Kevin could hear a soft, chanting music. It gradually grew louder until he suddenly knew what it was: that strange singing they always played on television when talking about monks. And now he could see them, a vast congregation of monks!

He seemed to be looking at them through flickering firelight. Gazing round, he saw that the whole abbey was now lit by flaming

torches that glowed and smoked in the dark.

And it *was* the whole abbey! This was no ruin, but a massive pillared cathedral. Kevin drew in a deep shuddery breath. He felt his throat go tight. What was happening? Where were Mum and Dad? What should he do?

He looked over to the first monk, and saw with horror that he was moving quickly towards him, stretching out and shaking a thin white hand at him. As he came nearer Kevin saw that he had a hood over his pale face.

Except that he had no face—only a grinning, bony whiteness with two dark eye-sockets.

Kevin turned and ran. He ran through the chanting monks, brushing against their black robes and trying not to see their skull-white faces and the blind sockets.

As he ran, turning and twisting, he bumped and stumbled against pillars that rose new and strong up to the roof, pillars he knew had fallen and crumbled away hundreds of years ago.

Now the monk was chasing him, making threatening noises but using no words that Kevin could understand. Out of breath from running and panic, he gasped and the torch smoke caught in his throat. The sweat on his forehead and between his shoulder-blades was chilled by air that was made cold by

night, or winter, or death—which one Kevin dared not guess.

He was trying to find that west doorway, the one the sun had shone through in another time from this, his own time. But he knew he was lost. It had not been built yet.

He ran, sobbing and panting, down an endless broad aisle. The torches threw moving shadows of the soaring pillars across the side aisles—aisles he had never seen before. He turned his head this way and that, searching for a way out, but saw only the long shadow of the monk overtaking him.

Then he caught sight of a door! Too massive to fit the arch that Kevin remembered, this was an enormous, heavy wooden door. It was fastened with a huge latch, broader than Kevin's arm. As he strained against it, the hooded shadow fell on the latch and his struggling hands. He pushed desperately against the door's mighty weight, and it slowly swung open. He burst through, just as a bony hand clawed at the back of his tee-shirt.

He was in a strange courtyard. But already the air was fresher, the singing fainter, the darkness greying into light. He looked back at the great doorway, and saw the monk standing framed against the dying glow of the torches. The dark figure was blurring, the deathly face now a white smudge. Then the doorway, and the towering abbey itself, wavered and dissolved into time-softened ruins.

He wanted only to get far, far away from this place. Where was the bank with Mum and Dad waiting?

There they were, waving at him—why had he not seen them before? He rushed over to them, still breathless from his terrified running.

"It's OK, we're not in that much of a hurry, Kev," said Dad, grabbing his hand as he clambered over the railings. "We did try to call you, but you seemed so far away."

Yeah, you could say that, thought Kevin, but out loud he said, "I couldn't find them after all."

"No, that's what we were trying to tell you. We could see them on the table in the ticket office. Can't think how they got there—the man left with us, didn't he?"

They had to come back the next day to collect the glasses, although Kevin refused to get out of the car. Mum said he was rude and ungrateful. She couldn't understand when Kevin said he was scared someone would recognize him.

In the end Dad was right—the photograph wasn't very good. The shaft of sun was too bright, making the rest of the picture too dark. It was Mum who made out the figure standing in the shadows.

"He looks a real weirdo, all in black, doesn't he? I don't remember anyone like that, do you Kev?" she said.

"Yeah," said Kevin, "as a matter of fact I do."

Bev's Story:

Bee for Bev

Bev's mother said she should be called Greta Garbo.

It was meant to be a joke. Greta Garbo was a film star who went around saying, "I vant to be alone" in a sexy foreign voice.

Bev liked to be alone. Her mother couldn't understand this.

They had moved into the country because it was cheaper than anywhere else. They found a cottage that was too old to be called modern or convenient, and not old enough to be called quaint or fashionable. That meant no one else wanted it, so it was cheap.

They couldn't afford to buy a car, not yet, so they had to use the three buses a day that served the nearby village. That made it difficult to see friends. Her mother was lonely—but Bev liked it.

Bev liked making things and she liked watching things. And she liked to do both alone. If she couldn't be outside, she was just as happy in her room, which was cluttered with models she had made out of paper kits.

All sorts of flying objects hung from the ceiling—mobiles and butterflies and planes—and the top of the chest was covered with dusty paper castles.

But today she was outside, watching things. She lay on her tummy watching a greeny-black beetle stubbornly push its way through the tall stalks. It hadn't rained for ages, and she could feel the spiky brown grass through her jeans. All round her in the field she could hear and see insects working among the clover and daisies.

Her mother had gone to do the Saturday shopping. Bev usually helped her carry it, but today the weather was so perfect that Mum had said she could stay at home. She had a pair of binoculars with her which had once belonged to her grandpa. They were old-fashioned and heavy, but if she propped her elbows on the ground she could manage them. Binoculars were specially good for watching things.

The field where Bev was lying, behind the house, sloped down to a valley. There was a reservoir there, an enormous lake which provided water for two big cities. On fine days people came there to fish, or picnic, or play cricket on its banks. At the foot of the field a narrow road led to the reservoir, and sometimes Bev played at counting how many cars went past in, say, ten minutes.

A noisy flock of sparrows, fluttering in and out of the barley field next door, caught her eye. She let the beetle go home and picked up the binoculars. She giggled to herself. The sparrows, yacketing away in an excited twitter, reminded her of the girls at her new school. She hadn't really bothered to get to know them yet. After fumbling for a moment with the focussing, she found the birds, then slowly tracked the hedge between the fields, down the hill little by little to the road.

That was queer: there seemed to be some kind of hold-up by the farthest bend. Two or three cars were waiting in a line. Perhaps there was going to be a traffic jam. She would try counting the cars as they collected.

The one at the back was blasting on his horn. Idiot, thought Bev, it wouldn't matter if he had to wait a few minutes on a lovely day like this.

She swung the glasses back to the first car at the bend. It was one of those sports cars whose roofs fold back—the sort where the wind is supposed to thrill through your hair but would in fact, in Bev's opinion, make such a mess of it that even Mum's fierce tuggings wouldn't get a comb through. Bev had no time for pretty wind-tossed curls. She tried to see what kind of hair-dos the sports car people had, but they looked so strange and peculiar she thought something must have happened to the binoculars.

Bev tried turning the focus, but it didn't help. She had a sudden prickly feeling in her own hair, as if some ants had crawled up into it. The two people in the car weren't moving at all. They looked all floppy and crumpled up and shrunken.

Something awful must have happened. Then she heard a scream. It was a scream of terror loud enough to reach her up the hill. Bev jumped to her feet.

A man got out of the car behind and stood holding the open door as he looked upwards. And then Bev, too, saw it. She didn't need her binoculars—it was as if she were staring through a magnifying glass in her own head.

Hovering over the cars was a bee. Its shadow lay dark over the sun-lit road.

It was an enormous horror of a bee. Light glinted off its great window-pane eyes, and wind from its sweeping shining wings lifted the man's hair. It was a monster bee, huge and hairy. As Bev gazed at it, the engine-drone of its wings drove it right over the man. A long black tongue darted out and probed at his head and face.

Up there alone on her hill, Bev shuddered. She gave a little moan and flung her hand over her mouth as she watched what happened next. The man stood quite still for a moment, then gently folded up. He

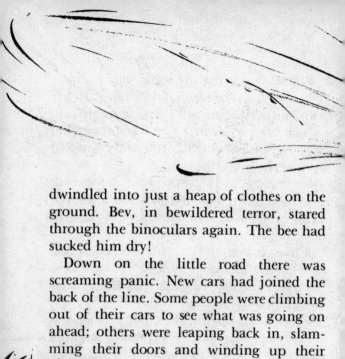

dwindled into just a heap of clothes on the ground. Bev, in bewildered terror, stared through the binoculars again. The bee had sucked him dry!

Down on the little road there was screaming panic. New cars had joined the back of the line. Some people were climbing out of their cars to see what was going on ahead; others were leaping back in, slamming their doors and winding up their

windows. A few were frantically trying to reverse and turn, skidding, grinding and shouting as they found their way blocked by other cars.

The bee had settled on one car. It squatted menacingly on the roof, its long, thin, jointed legs gripping each side. Its tongue flickered over the windscreen.

Bev looked round wildly. Was she the only person to be watching all this? Was she completely alone? Could no one else see and help those people? But all round her the countryside drowsed in its summer haze.

Oh please, please, let me think, she whispered. I do know about bees, don't I, I've watched them, haven't I, only . . . Only they were small and bumbly and funny, not nightmare monsters.

She remembered feeling sorry for them. Why? That was it! If a bee stung something, it would always die, because its little hooked sting dragged out some of the bee's body as it flew away.

She had an idea—well, it was worth a try.

She tried not to think what this giant's sting would look like, as she turned and ran hard back home up the hill.

She rushed through the quiet, empty kitchen upstairs to her room, and dragged a chair over to the corner. Its legs caught against the bed legs, then knocked against the chest, so that models shook and fell down. Bev sobbed in fear and frustration. She stood on the chair and reached up to one of her hanging treasures. She couldn't reach the drawing pin in the ceiling, so she tugged at the string till it broke free.

It was a big bee, a jolly bee, a laughing black-and-yellow bee. It was made out of that frilly paper that folds up like a concertina, making a flat pack instead of a round, plump, bee.

Bev tore out of the house and down the sloping field. Please let it work, make it work—over and over in her mind went the words. About three-quarters of the way down she stopped, her breath juddering through her.

She raised her lovely frilled bee into the air. Straining till her ribs ached, she pointed it at the road and hurled it into the air.

It seemed to hang there for a second. Then

a breath of wind caught it and drifted it towards the cars.

The gleaming eyes must have seen it. The monster rose in the air and turned to face the stranger. Whatever it thought it saw through all the hundred edges of those eyes, it decided to fight. It grasped the paper body with its grotesque insect legs. It grappled with it, crushed it and forced it to the ground. A cruel and easy victory.

But when it rose again, it was flying awkwardly, dazedly. Trailing from its body was a sticky, moist spill of guts. It flew zig-zagging towards the lake, and the deep drone of its wings was uneven and broken. Then, somewhere behind the raised bank of the reservoir, the noise stopped.

Bev found she had been holding her breath. Her knees and stomach muscles were trembling as she stumbled back up the hill. She pushed open the back door and sat down heavily at the kitchen table. She laid her head on her arms. She could hear the cooker clock softly ticking in the empty quietness.

And then, suddenly, there was her mother calling as she came through the front hall. "Sorry I'm late, love! The traffic was *crawling* on the way home."

It was good not to be alone any more.

Ginger's Story:

Dummy Run

Ginger was a bit of a villain at the best of times, but today he was being really terrible. He knew it. He was enjoying it.

He and Trish and Chubs were shopping. He normally didn't mind shopping, not if it were for sensible things like new trainers or the latest pack of football cards. But today was *disgustingly* boring. (Disgusting was his latest word, which he used as often and as rudely as he could.)

Trish was looking for a new dress for the Christmas disco. Trish was his big sister, and she'd been fed up before they had even started because Mum had made her take Ginger and Chubs with her. "Chubs" sounds like a dog, but actually he was Ginger's disgusting baby brother. Ginger had decided that if everyone could call him Ginger, because he had (you guessed it) red hair, then he would be just as boring and call the baby Chubs, because he

was (you guessed it again) disgustingly fat.

They were in a big department store, on the floor below the street. This was where Trish reckoned all the "in" clothes would be—that meant the ones everyone else would be wearing. There was disgusting music coming from the speakers all round them.

Trish pointed to Chubs in his pushchair. "See to him for me, will you?" she said.

Ginger sighed. He stood there for a while, first on one leg, then the other, leaning over the handles of the pushchair so that the whole thing nearly tipped up.

"Honestly Ginger, can't you do anything right?" Trish said, then disappeared into a little room with a curtain instead of a door, and all Ginger could see were her feet without her shoes. He sighed again. The afternoon was going to be just as disgusting as he had said it would be.

He started to push Chubs around, in and out of the racks of dresses and blouses and baggy trousers. Somewhere behind them he heard Trish calling through the music. She sounded puzzled and angry. He speeded up, making racing-car noises, and popped out from behind a rack right beside her.

"I'm gonna tell Mum if you don't pack it in!" Trish hissed at him, embarrassed at having to call out for him. He sniggered, and rolled his eyes up in the way he knew drove her stark, staring, disgustingly, mad.

Trish looked for one moment as if she would thump him, but instead she shrugged her shoulders and went back into the changing room. Ginger looked down at Chubs. He didn't need looking after, anyway, for he'd gone to sleep, flopped over sideways with one fat little arm hanging out of the pushchair. How disgusting, thought Ginger, and walked away.

He wandered back through the racks of clothes, in and out, left and right, until he came to some big swing doors. It would be a lot cooler out there, and quieter too. He would go out for just a minute, and, anyway, Trish would be ages yet. He leaned against one of the doors, but had to push it very hard before it opened. It closed quickly and heavily behind him.

He was alone on the landing of a wide stone staircase with a metal bannister and railings twisting round and round its middle. Should he go up? No, too far. He was already below street level so it would be easier to go down. At the head of the stairs there was a notice saying *Staff Only*. Ginger decided that was to stop some old lady struggling all the way down for nothing, and didn't mean Keep Out. Anyway, there was no one around to see what he did.

Sliding the palm of his hand against the

wall behind him as he went (not that he was scared, but the wall felt good and solid), he ran down to the next landing. He followed the wall round and went more slowly down the next lot of steps.

The air really was fresher here, almost chilly, and quieter without that music. In fact, all he could hear were his own feet. It was darker, too, with only the light from above shining weakly down the stairwell.

Then he was at the bottom, on a level that might be a corridor, or a store room, only he couldn't quite see in the dusky light. By now it must be properly dark outside, and Ginger was surprised at the slightly tight feeling in his chest that came with the thought. After all, it was almost dark when he came out of school these days, and that didn't worry him.

Be stupid to come down this far and not look around, he thought, moving away from the wall. Not that there seemed much to see— pretty disgusting, really. And it would be even more stupid to be caught down here when the shop closed. Better go back, just in case.

As he turned he glimpsed something pale out of the corner of his eye. He stopped and peered through the gloom. Over there, by the far wall, there seemed to be faint shapes. They were like the dim outlines of—well, people. And what was that scraping noise? He stood quite still to listen—and realized how fast his heart was beating.

Just then he felt a touch on his shoulder. It was a hand.

Ginger's breath sucked itself in with a great whoosh, and he spun round. Someone was there beside him in the grey light. Someone with no clothes at all. Worse, with no hair either, just a smooth pale head.

Ginger twisted round again. There was another, harder to make out, because this time the skin was dark, dark all over with the same smooth bald head. In total panic now, he twirled round and saw more of them moving stiffly towards him. Shuffle, shuffle. Shuffle, shuffle. Steadily, steadily, they came towards him.

Ginger was so frightened his heart and stomach seemed to be beating against each other. He could hear his own quick breathing—and a kind of scratchy squeak as their arms moved jerkily up and out to reach him.

One of them snatched at his woolly hat, the special hat in United's colours that he always wore. Then they closed in.

They all had the same blank faces, staring and expressionless. One or two were dark brown, but most had an eerily unreal pinky-flesh colour, and their fingers and arms were cold and hard and bruising as they knocked awkwardly against him. Ginger stood still with terror as they swayed round him.

One pulled at his scarf, so that it tightened round his neck. Another groped with stiff, arched fingers at his hair, scraping and tugging it. His anorak was roughly pulled from behind. Then one of them started to twist his arm backwards and forwards as if expecting it to separate at the elbow. As the movements became more and more impatient, Ginger realized it was no longer quiet.

They were talking to each other.

They spoke in short bursts, and their growly, scratchy voices echoed against the stone walls and floor.

"Left its clothes on."

"And its hair."

"They're not new."

"Never red hair."

"Christmas window."

"Can't stay here with clothes on."

"Nor a wig."

"Bad mover."

"A child."

"Neglected. Gone stiff."

"Always at Christmas."

"Get it off."

"Sent down here like that."

"Disgusting."

It was Ginger's word, and it saved him.

Suddenly he was much less frightened and much more angry. So angry, in fact, he felt sobs rising in his throat till it ached with fury.

"Let go, let go! That hurts, that really hurts! You're mean, you're wrong, you're stupid idiots! *You're* the dummies, not me!"

In a tantrum of rage he turned and whirled, kicking and beating with his fists against their hard, unyielding bodies.

And they fell back. They fell back stiffly, knocking each other as they rolled with strange surprised grunts on to the stone floor. There they sprawled, one with its arm no longer elegant, pointing queerly upwards, another with its head at a weird angle, some with a leg or two horridly cut off at the knee, another with a foot twisted to face backwards . . .

Ginger didn't wait to be sorry, didn't wait even to pick up his special hat. He tore up the stairs. How many flights had he come down? Was it this landing or the next? Then he heard the music once more, and saw the big swing doors. Gasping with relief, he pushed to let himself in.

At first all he saw among the brightness of the lights and the clothes was a group of shop ladies in their dark blue skirts bending over someone. Wiping his eyes with his knuckles, he came a little closer.

It was Trish! Big bossy Trish, sitting on a

chair, crying! One of the ladies was rocking Chubs's pushchair, back and forth, back and forth, but he was still bawling, red-faced with misery, as he watched Trish.

Ginger ran forward without thinking. He pushed through the ladies and flung himself down against Trish's knees. She squealed and grabbed him by the shoulders.

"Ginger! Oh Ginger, I'll *murder* you when we get home!"

But Ginger looked up at her face, blurry through his tears, and smiled. He knew he was in no danger now.

Jacqueline's Story

Brewing Trouble

The other children were scared of Jacqueline.

Jacqueline was a big girl for her age, bigger than all the boys, and she didn't mind barging and pushing—and sometimes pinching in a really sore way—to get a good place in the dinner line, or bag a desk by the window, or grab the newest, bounciest netball.

Jacqueline told tales. "Miss, Jason keeps taking my felt tips", or, "Sir, Morris and Rashid were fighting at playtime". Sometimes she even told lies. "Miss, Emma pulled my hair", when in fact Emma would never dare touch Jacqueline's hair for fear of what she might do to her later.

Jacqueline boasted. "I've got my own

television in my bedroom", or, "I'm going to get a new bicycle—it costs £150"! The other children didn't really believe her, but they were never quite sure. They could see, from her neat little calculator and all the sweets in her pocket and the films she said she'd seen, that she got most things she wanted.

Jacqueline knew how to hurt people's feelings. She asked Hing Ling why her eyes were all funny. She jeered when Juan couldn't say a new English word. She said Darren must be a greedy pig to be so fat. She said Thomas's father couldn't love him or he wouldn't have gone away. It was cruel and untrue, and the children knew it, but no one stuck up for Hing Ling or Juan or Darren or Thomas, because they were frightened of what Jacqueline might say next to *them*.

Jacqueline was clever. Perhaps that was the worst part, and why no one knew how to deal with her. Everyone sat very quiet when Jacqueline's drawings, poems and stories were pinned on the wall. Everyone tried not to notice that Jacqueline always did harder projects than the rest of them. Everyone stared stonily when Jacqueline had to show the P.E. class how to climb a rope. She seemed best at everything.

Except swimming.

Friday was swimming day, when they all trailed in a long line of twos to the local swimming baths for a special swimming instructor to teach them. No one wanted to be Jacqueline's partner, but Jacqueline did the picking and you didn't argue with Jacqueline.

Miss Raffles was the swimming teacher's name, and she was *fierce*. She wore a navy blue track suit and had a whistle on a string round her neck. She blew it, and waved, and pointed, and shouted, and stamped her white plimsolls, and took no notice of what anyone said—including Jacqueline.

Jacqueline was hopeless at swimming. And Jacqueline hated being hopeless at anything. At first she tried different ways of getting out of the lesson: she'd made her mother write notes saying she had a cold, or bad ears, or had hurt her elbow, and sometimes she left her swimming things at home, accidentally-on-purpose. If it had been anyone but Jacqueline, people would have said she was scared. It was certainly clear that Jacqueline hated the water.

Then Miss Raffles asked their class teacher to write to Jacqueline's mother, and after that, whatever the letter said, she had gone swimming with everyone else.

Miss Raffles had no time for people who hung about, or wouldn't jump in when they were told, or didn't like putting their face in the water. People like Jacqueline, in fact. She wasn't the only one, but because she was a big, strong girl, Miss Raffles seemed to think she should be trying harder.

"Hurry up, Jacqueline!"

"Well, don't just stand there, Jacqueline!"

"For goodness' sake, child, pull yourself together!"

So Jacqueline slogged across the width of the pool, chin stretched out of the water, head swinging clumsily from side to side, with gasping breath and aching legs. If she had been anyone else you might have felt sorry for her. But it was as unthinkable to feel sorry for Jacqueline as it would be to call her Jacquie. It simply never occurred to anyone.

Then one day she gave up floundering across the pool. She walked through the water to the bath edge and started to heave herself out.

"And what do you think you're doing?" It was Miss Raffles, sharp-eyed as ever, standing over her. "Oh no you don't, my girl, not till I say so!" And she put her hand on Jacqueline's head and pushed her back into the water.

Instantly the class stopped squealing and splashing, and turned in silence to watch.

It was too much, it seemed, for Jacqueline, to feel everyone's eyes on her like that. She clung to the edge of the pool and cried, the tears running down her wet face into the corners of her mouth. Then they heard what she was saying.

"You wait!" she muttered. "I'll get you for this, you'll see. You just wait!"

The class knew you didn't try nonsense like that on Miss Raffles.

"That's it! That's enough!" she shouted.

"Out! Out you come! Right, go and stand over there until I tell you". No one had ever seen Miss Raffles quite as angry as this.

At first it looked as if Jacqueline were going to obey. For a few moments she stood shivering and shaking and dripping on the tiled floor, hugging her arms round herself and staring at her toes.

Then, quite suddenly, she seemed to make up her mind about something, and marched straight out of the pool into the changing rooms. She didn't come back.

And the day Miss Raffles took on Jacqueline was probably when it all began.

The following week Jacqueline was strangely quiet, almost dreamy. She was even ticked off for gazing out of the window instead of getting on with her sums. It was a peaceful change for the rest of the class, yet it seemed so unnatural that they felt uneasy.

The only lesson in the entire week when Jacqueline seemed to concentrate with her old fierce energy was—of all things—Cooking. Usually it was a class everyone enjoyed. There was always such a nice smell connected with it, and Mrs Dean, the teacher, made each person feel they were a kitchen genius. Each week, everyone had to bring either some money or some ingredients, and they would each make slight variations of the same thing. Within reason, they were allowed to chat to each other, and everyone regarded it as fun, never as hard work.

This week they made biscuits. Everyone mixed and kneaded and pummelled the same basic dough. They had each chosen their own flavours—lemon, chocolate, cinnamon, orange, ginger . . . They were supposed to have washed their hands, but one or two grey lumps of dough looked as if they might be flavoured with ink or playground dust.

Jacqueline had brought her own flavour from home. She refused to let anyone see it, or to say what it was. "Mind your own business," she had growled at Emma, when she chattily asked.

Mrs Dean moved among them, handing out fancy shapes to cut the biscuits. Jacqueline refused to take any.

Mrs Dean hovered. There was something about Jacqueline's concentrated scowl that unnerved her. There was really no need for the child to take it all so *seriously*.

"What was your flavour again, Jacqueline?" she asked in a friendly way, to ease the tension.

Jacqueline looked up into her eyes, very direct. "Powdered centipede", she answered abruptly. For a second Mrs Dean looked taken aback. Then she seemed to decide it was a little joke, and smiled faintly. But Emma, who had glimpsed Jacqueline take from her pocket a little twist of paper, like the ones you find in packets of potato crisps, was not so sure.

Everyone but Jacqueline cut out their biscuits into pretty shapes. She, hunched over her rolled-out dough, was cutting out a large single shape with a penknife. She was breathing hard and muttering to herself. When they all carefully eased their crescents, stars and hearts on to the baking trays, they saw Jacqueline's single enormous biscuit. It was in the shape of a person.

What they didn't see was Jacqueline, standing close by the cooker, turning up the oven heat.

It was the smell of burning that alerted Mrs Dean. The children had cleared away and washed up, and returned to their classroom, leaving their biscuits to finish baking. With a puzzled frown, Mrs Dean bent down to open the oven. Bitter, eye-stinging heat billowed into her face.

Exclaiming with angry bewilderment, Mrs Dean looked down at the scorched brown biscuits. Another few moments and they would have been thoroughly burnt. The children were going to be so upset when they returned at dinnertime to see their results. How could it possibly have happened?

Later she sympathised with the children, and apologised. But she was unprepared for Jacqueline's fury.

"The child practically threw a tantrum!" she told the staffroom that afternoon. "She picked up her ridiculous biscuit man, or whatever it was, and *flung* it in the waste bin. She really is a very odd girl!"

Jacqueline showed no interest at all when, on Friday, Miss Raffles turned up at the swimming baths with both hands bandaged. The rest of the class buzzed with amazement when Miss Raffles told them she had been rescued only just in time from a fire in her flat. She had burnt her hands quite badly, so she couldn't hold her whistle.

"Still," she said in her brisk way, "that won't hold us up, will it?"

Jacqueline turned her head away, as if bored with the whole business. No one saw the stony look of hatred on her face.

Jacqueline took no notice of her classmates or her teachers in the following days. Her mind seemed farther and farther away from what was happening round her. When at one point the teacher spoke sharply to her about paying attention, Jacqueline turned such a cold blank stare on her that she almost shuddered. What a creepy child! she found herself thinking.

The children left Jacqueline alone. They steered clear of her as they rushed round the playground, and never sat beside her at table. No one said anything, but they all knew there was something eerie about Jacqueline.

Jacqueline didn't mind, or didn't notice. Only in Cooking did she come alive again. It seemed to be the only important moment in the week for her.

This time they were making spaghetti bolognese. They all cut up different things, the onions, the carrots, the celery, the tomatoes. But playtime came in the middle, and Mrs Dean needed only two or three to stay behind to stir the mixture in the saucepans. She picked two from the forest of waving arms, and then felt compelled to turn to the silent Jacqueline. She didn't have her hand up, but was simply staring at Mrs Dean through narrowed eyes. The teacher found herself pointing at her. "Right, that makes three," she said.

Throughout break, Jacqueline's head was bent over her pan. She stirred and mumbled and tested with intense concentration.

Ten minutes later, the other two were loudly sniffing the air.

"Ugh, what a horrible pong! It's like rotten fish!"

"Yuk! More like a blocked drain."

"All right, you two, that's enough." Mrs Dean walked over to Jacqueline's saucepan. "That really does smell pretty foul. What on earth have you got in it?"

Once again, Jacqueline looked up into her eyes, very direct.

"Two grams of frogspawn, the eyes of four bluebottles, pinch of grated rat's claw, three slugs, a ferret's tail and just a touch of—"

"That'll do, Jacqueline." It was too much for even Mrs Dean. "It wasn't very funny the last time. Now whatever you think you're playing at, it smells absolutely disgusting and you will kindly take it out to the girls' toilets and flush it away. *And* you will pay for the wasted ingredients."

She turned to the other two, expecting them to be giggling at a joke gone wrong. But they weren't. They simply stood there, spoons in hand, watching Jacqueline strolling unconcernedly from the room. They looked at each other, then at Mrs Dean. She could have sworn they looked scared.

"She won't throw it away, you know, Miss" said one of them.

"Don't be silly! What else can she do with it?"

"Dunno, Miss. You can't ever tell with Jacqueline."

There was no swimming that Friday. In morning assembly the Head told them, in a hushed voice, that Miss Raffles had been taken very suddenly ill with some kind of food poisoning. And that, very tragically and unexpectedly, she had died. The Head knew it would be a great shock for everyone.

Only Jacqueline was not shocked. She was gazing out of the window and if anyone had looked at her they would have seen her small, satisfied smile.

Cathy's Story

Framed!

"Goodnight,
Sleep tight,
Don't let the bugs bite.
If they do,
Squeeze them tight—
Night-night."

Dad always said that. He said his mother used to say it to him. One part of Cathy thought it was silly, but the other part of her loved it. Besides, it was a useful way of keeping him with her a little while longer, especially when he was going out, like tonight.

"Don't go yet—you haven't said goodnight to Mischief."

"G'night Mischief."

"And Teddy."

"Oh come on, Catkins!"

"Didn't *you* have toys you took to bed?"

"You know I did—we've talked about this hundreds of times. Though not as many toys as you, you daft hap'orth!" He grinned, and jabbed at her with his finger through the bedclothes. "But look, I've got to go, or Dave will think I'm not coming."

Dave was Cathy's older brother, and tonight was Parents Evening at his school.

That meant she would be alone—well, almost. Mrs Davies from next door had come round, and was already sitting comfortably with a cup of tea in front of the TV.

"I don't like it when you're both out," Cathy said.

"Rubbish! You get on O.K. with Mrs Davies, don't you? Course you do! Come on now, give us a kiss and then I'm off."

She hooked her arms round his neck and hauled him down to her. He laughed, then gave her a shattering kiss in her ear which made her squeal and let go.

"Leave the door open," she called after him as he left.

She heard him saying something quickly to Mrs Davies, and the sound of the front door closing. Then there was nothing to hear but some stupid TV audience laughing.

Usually Cathy liked the noise of the television in the background when she went to sleep. But everything felt different tonight. She was restless, and couldn't sleep. She re-arranged her animals several times. She kicked off her quilt because she was hot, then pulled it back on because she was cold. She tried to picture Dad at the school.

At Cathy's school the teachers liked to talk to the parents without the children being there to hear, so she wasn't very sure what went on at Parents Evening. She imagined teachers showing off the best of the children's work, and giving a conducted tour of the classroom mixed up with a kind of end-of-term report.

Cathy giggled and looked round her own room. She put on a fancy voice and pretended to be a teacher—pretending and dreaming had somehow become more important to her since Mum had gone.

"Now here's a picture of Bonfire Night which Cathy painted. She's quite capable of good work if she would only pay attention."

"Here's a collection of dolls from different countries. Cathy made two of them herself—quite neatly done, I think, considering Mike Henson had them stuffed in his shoebag for three days."

"This is a Bronze Swimming Certificate—Cathy does try hard at sports, even if she is not always successful. Next to it is a Grade One flute certificate. What a pity Cathy didn't continue with that—the school is so proud of its orchestra, you know."

She was running out of things she had done herself. But she was enjoying the game, so she carried on anyway.

"Now two pictures that are among our favourites. One is a very pretty picture of a little boy fishing by a river bank. The other one . . ." Cathy stopped suddenly.

She stared at the other picture that hung on

the wall at the end of her bed. She forgot to be a teacher and just stared and stared.

It was different tonight. Surely it was different? She knew the picture so well. She had looked at it so many times. *Something* was different about it, she was certain.

It was a romantic picture—Dave always said it was wet. There was a very grand house, with a beautiful garden with trees stretching in front of it. There was a flight of steps up to a front entrance with graceful columns on either side, like one of those stately homes you could visit. There was a man and a lady in old-fashioned clothes—the lady was wearing a full cloak over her long skirt. The man was coming through the door and was holding out one hand towards the lady standing on the top step.

At least, that was what Cathy had always thought they were doing. Only now, tonight, they were . . . Oh, you're just being *silly!* she told herself sharply, like her pretend-teacher. Whatever she had once thought they were doing, tonight the man had come right out on to the top step, and the lady was standing at the bottom, looking back up at him. The man's other arm was raised, and he was waving a whip.

How could she be so wrong about a picture she saw every day? But there it was, right in front of her, not at all like she thought.

She checked back on the fishing picture. But it looked just as it had always looked. Perhaps it was because she liked the little boy fishing best that she hadn't looked properly at the house picture before. Maybe it was true that she didn't pay enough attention to things.

Cathy smiled at the boy, but he had his back to her, thinking hard about his fish. Now you really are bonkers, she thought, smiling at pictures! But it was a happy dreamy picture, and it made her feel good. A little boat was drawn up against the river bank, overhung with drooping branches whose leaves made soft shadows on the water. The boy was fishing from the end of the boat. You couldn't see the other bank, so it must have been a wide river, but the boy looked safe and content.

It was a drowsy summer's day picture, and, gazing at it, Cathy at last fell asleep.

When she woke up the next morning, there was a cold, no-nonsense light seeping through the curtains. She remembered her funny feeling about the house picture. She looked at it carefully, then shivered with excitement.

It had changed again, it really had! The lady was no longer looking at the man. She had turned and was gathering her cloak around her. The man looked as if he were going to follow her down the steps.

59

Cathy was thrilled. This was going to be fun, her own special secret. She wondered what could happen next.

And, yes, at first it was fun. Every night before she went to sleep, and every morning when she woke up, the picture had changed. But she never actually saw the people moving, not once. The lady left the steps and started to cross the lawn. The man came down the steps after her.

And then Cathy began to feel just a little afraid. Because, as they came closer to the front of the picture, she could see their faces. The lady was as pretty as Cathy had always imagined—but her wide blue eyes were terrified. The man following her was tall and very dark, with big broad shoulders. His bushy eyebrows were scowling at the lady.

They moved very, very gradually, a little every day. It was like watching the slowest of slow-motion replays on television. At the same time the picture was giving off a stronger and stronger sense of fear. Cathy knew that there was something very dangerous about that big man.

Once she tried to tell Dave or Dad what was happening. But as she was leaving the room to find them, something made her glance over her shoulder at the picture. And she saw the man glaring straight at her. He was *willing* her to come back, and she found she

had to. She sat on the edge of her bed and tried
to quieten the quivery feeling in her stomach.
Yes, he was dangerous.

As the days and nights went past, the lady ran more and more desperately from the man, crossing and re-crossing the lawn, hiding behind trees and a trellis of roses. But where could she go? There was no escape from him, coming closer and closer to her, with that cruel whip raised in his hand, and his black eyes fierce and angry.

Cathy longed to know why he was so angry. What had the lady done? Nothing bad, Cathy was sure of that. She was sure, too, that there was something sinister and wicked in the man.

Cathy was scared. She had seen the man's eyes looking at her, and she knew that in some way she and the lady shared the same danger. She had to try and save them both.

Sometimes she was too frightened to sleep. She would stare at the picture, daring the man to hurt the lady while she was watching. She wished she knew what to do.

One night the lady reached the frame of the picture, and was leaning against it, her head bowed over in despair. Cathy was frantic. How could she rescue her? Where could the lady go? Then the answer seemed to float into her mind: *into another picture!* Cathy had only one other picture, but, yes, that was it!

She scrambled to the end of the bed. Would she be in time? Would the man guess what she was doing?

She stood on the bed to unhook the house picture, and on a chair to reach the other one. Then she propped them up on the chest of drawers, leaning against the wall, side by side with their frames touching. She hoped the lady would understand. She knew *he* would, and would be racing to stop her.

She woke very early next morning and at once knew something very important was going on. Then her sleepy mind cleared. She looked over anxiously at the two pictures.

The lady had understood! Cathy gazed at her lovely fishing picture, her happy, sunny picture, and saw with a rush of joy that the boy was rowing his boat over the wide river right to the far edge of the picture. And sitting with him, laughing so prettily, was Cathy's lady.

The man stood helpless by the frame of his own picture. Without a boat he could never reach them. The whip hung limply by his side, but his face was tight with rage. As Cathy looked at him, he slowly turned his head. Their eyes met. At last she had seen him move.

She picked up the picture and tiptoed into Dad's bedroom. It would be better there. A picture of a man and a house was boring, anyway.

Peter's Story

Uncle Charlie's Game

Peter first saw the creature one hot summer afternoon, on his way home from school.

Afterwards, he wondered what had made him look up, because the creature itself had made no sound.

Peter had been moodily kicking a stone along the dusty lane, not even looking where he was going. He was thinking that there was no fun in going home these days, not now Uncle Charlie had come to stay.

He knew that his mother would probably be out. She collected his sister Tracy from the infant school in the village, and just lately had begun to stay on for a cup of tea with one of the other mothers. Perhaps she too did not want to go home. His father would be working in the fields somewhere. The house would be empty—except for Uncle Charlie.

So Peter was not hurrying. He stopped under the big oak tree that marked a bend in the lane and put his case down. Thursdays was his violin day. He was proud of his violin, and even enjoyed practising in the evenings—at least he had until Uncle Charlie had come—but the heavy case did bite into his hand after he had been carrying it for a while. Especially when it was hot.

He stood in the pool of shade from the tree, and then glanced up. The sun flickered through the leaves, dappling them and the dark branches with little patches of brightness.

It was the movement of the tail that caught his eye. The black tip was twitching gently from side to side. The rest of the body was quite still, dappled golden like the tree. Without the twitching tail, Peter would have missed it.

The creature stared silently at Peter through half-closed eyes. For a moment it seemed as if the only thing in the world that was moving was that black-tipped tail. Then Peter ran.

He ran and ran. The winter mud, churned into ridges and hollows by cows and tractors, had now dried hard and knobbly, and Peter stumbled and nearly fell several times before he reached his own gate. Only then did he

stop and look behind him—and realized he had left his violin case in the road.

His mother was puzzled when she and Tracy found it later. And a little angry, too.

"Those things cost money, you know. I had to sign a form for the school saying we'd be responsible for it. What on earth got into you? You don't just leave violins lying around in the road!" And so on. Uncle Charlie, of course, joined in.

"Violins!" he said scornfully. "Scrape, scrape, scrape! Load of rubbish, in my opinion—boy ought to be out doing something useful, if you ask me."

No one had asked him. Peter and his mother exchanged glances and stopped talking. Peter had been going to tell her about the strange creature, but he couldn't bring himself to mention it in front of Uncle Charlie. He guessed his mother disliked Uncle Charlie as much as he did.

Uncle Charlie was his father's uncle—so really he was Peter's great-uncle. He had gone to Africa long ago as a soldier, and settled there. He had had servants and a big house—far grander than he could have dreamed of if he had stayed in England. When the country he lived in became independent, he was so horrified he came back to England.

He no longer had any friends or family in

England, except his nephew, Peter's father. So he had asked if he could stay with them just until he found his feet. But time was passing, and Uncle Charlie didn't seem to be in any hurry to move.

Peter had had to give up his room to him and to move in with Tracy. His bedroom was now totally Uncle Charlie's: everywhere there were souvenirs of the old days in Africa,

when Uncle Charlie had helped rich tourists feel clever and brave by shooting big game animals. There were photographs of Uncle Charlie and his satisfied customers standing boastfully over a dead lion or buffalo. Rhino horns and elephant tusks were laid out on the dressing table. Peter thought they looked sad and out of place in this little English bedroom, so far from the great rolling plains of their homeland.

Uncle Charlie never tired of telling stories about his hunting adventures. He clearly thought Peter was a feeble sort of boy, a boy who liked music and reading and even took care not to tread on a beetle. Someone, he seemed to think, must toughen him up. But Peter didn't want to talk to him. He wouldn't even go into his old room. He hated what Uncle Charlie had done to it.

The worst thing of all was the rug. Across the floor was a leopard-skin, with the noble head and great teeth still snarling at one end, and the legs stretched out pathetically on either side. The black-tipped tail pointed lifelessly at the door, so that everyone who went into the room trod on it. Except Peter, who shuddered at the thought of standing on the dead fur.

It was the black-tipped tail that Peter had recognised. He tried to talk to his parents after supper, when Uncle Charlie had gone grumbling up the stairs. He was always grumbling. England, even in the summer, was too cold for him. He was used to servants doing everything for him, no matter how rudely he asked. He didn't like the food Peter's mother cooked. He was bored and lonely, but thought the company at the village pub was beneath him.

Tracy was in bed, and Peter was helping his mother with the washing-up. He started to tell her about the fright he had had, about the animal in the tree. But she only sighed impatiently.

"Oh Peter, don't *you* start! As if it isn't bad enough with *him*"—she jerked her head at the ceiling—"going on and on about his wretched animals. You've been listening to too many of his daft stories, you have. Fed up with them all, I am, and I don't want to hear no more!"

Peter thought she sounded close to tears. He looked at his father, who was leaning against the mantel-piece, knocking his pipe out on the empty fireplace. His father was a shy, gentle man, who seldom spoke. Peter could see he had no idea how to deal with the problem of his uncle. How could he turn him out? Yet how could he allow him to stay and go on upsetting everyone?

So Peter said no more, and even began to think that he had imagined the still, silent beast in the tree.

Then he saw it a second time.

It was a few weeks into the autumn term, when the evenings were beginning to shorten. Peter had stayed late for football practice, and so missed the school bus. He had taken the ordinary bus to the end of the village, and was walking home down the lane. The sun was low, casting long shadows of everything, the fences, the bushes and himself walking.

Peter was watching his lanky shadow stretching right across the road and up the bank on the other side, when he suddenly realized there was another shadow beside his. At that very moment he heard a sort of soft grunting cough. He gasped and wheeled round. Standing quite close to him was a full-grown leopard.

For a moment their eyes met: the boy's wide with terror and surprise, the leopard's a golden, unblinking stare. It stood calm, unmoving. Peter's heart seemed to leap into his throat, but before he could run away, the leopard had gone. How fast, how silently it must have moved!

Peter knew that this time he had to tell his father. After all, an animal like that would prey on calves and sheep and poultry. But when at last, chest heaving, out of breath, he found his father at the bottom of the field they called Five-Acre, he realized it was no use.

His father listened seriously to him. He was too kind a man to laugh. But then he ruffled his son's hair, and talked about dreams, and tricks of the light, and old newspaper stories about huge rogue dogs, and—of course—his uncle's hunting tales.

"I'd know if there were summat roaming wild round here," he said, "you can be sure of that, lad." He smiled fondly at his son, and sent him on home to get cleaned up for supper.

Peter felt frightened and bewildered. That night he dreamed of great cats with yellow eyes who stared at him while he struggled to run away. What was dream, and what was real?

He tried to talk to Uncle Charlie, to ask if he had ever seen a leopard here, down the lane? Uncle Charlie barked with laughter.

"A leopard, boy? Here, in England? Got too much sense," he muttered, as an afterthought. He was hating the colder days, and was staying more and more alone in his room, secretly burning the electric fire. Peter's mother, who always tried to put off lighting the fire downstairs till winter really began, was in despair over the heating bill.

"Besides, you don't often see leopards in daytime, you know. Fierce, cunning beasts. Not like the lion. Lazy devils, lions. Difficult to miss a lion, in fact, though you don't tell the customer that! But a leopard—that's different. Damn fine shooting, that's what stopped that fellow up in my room, you know, damn fine shooting." Uncle Charlie was off.

Peter looked at the grey moustache, the small pale eyes, watery now with age, but still cold and mean. Fine shooting, maybe, thought Peter, but the leopard didn't have a gun, did he?

Winter was drawing in when Peter saw the creature for the third time.

He was at the back door, trying to put the cat out after supper. But she wouldn't go. She dug her claws into the mat, and scrabbled and hissed and fought. He was bending down, gripping her with both hands, when he lifted his head to look out into the yard.

What he saw made him drop the cat. She shot between his legs back into the safety of the kitchen. Out there two gleaming green eyes shone in the darkness, caught in the shaft of light from the door. Peter had seen animals' eyes shining terrified in car headlights, but these were large and glowed quite unafraid.

He shouted. "Dad! Dad, come quick. It's here. You can see it, it's here!"

His father came, but not anxiously, not quickly enough. The creature had gone. Had it been the leopard? Was it out there now, watching, waiting?

Uncle Charlie had heard the shout. When they both came back into the warm bright living-room, he was looking up at them, his lip curled in a sneer.

"Your leopard come visiting again, eh boy? You're a rum one and no mistake. You don't take enough exercise, you know. That would knock the nonsense out of you. When I was your age I'd be out there potting a rabbit or two for my mother, or a crow, or setting my mole traps. Plenty of action for a lad in the country, you know, if you get your nose out of those books! Suppose you'll be scratching away on that instrument again in a moment? Don't know what your father's thinking of, letting a son of his fiddle his time away. Eh? Fiddle—hear that?" He stopped to enjoy his own joke.

A few weeks after that evening, Peter saw the leopard for the last time.

He was standing at the window of the room he shared with Tracy. It was an ordinary Saturday morning. His mother was shopping and had taken Tracy with her. His father was clearing ditches—Peter could just see his bent figure in the distance. Uncle Charlie was in his room. Saturdays was his library day, but he hadn't left yet. Everything was ordinary, like any other Saturday.

Then he saw the leopard. It was loping

round the edge of the garden, down by the hedge. Steadily, gracefully, pad pad pad, round the house. It was very clear. Anyone could see it.

He ran out of the room to shout for Uncle Charlie. He banged with his fist on Uncle Charlie's door.

"It's down there now, Uncle Charlie! I know it is! The leopard, Uncle Charlie—you can see it for yourself!"

Uncle Charlie opened his door. He was already wearing his coat and scarf, ready for his trip to the library.

"Stop making that racket, boy, for goodness' sake." He pushed past Peter to the stairs.

Peter trotted down the stairs close behind him.

"Don't go out now, Uncle Charlie—honestly, I did see it. It *was* a leopard, Uncle Charlie, don't go out there now!"

Uncle Charlie twitched his shoulder sharply, as if to shrug off an irritating fly. "Don't nag me, boy!" he said. "I've no time for your tom-fool game. I'm off to the library."

He opened the front door and started down the path towards the gate into the lane. Then Peter heard that growling, grunting cough.

By the hedge at the bottom of the lawn, the leopard waited.

It was crouching low, its head almost on

the ground, its tail swishing in angry jerks: flick, flick; flick, flick. Its mouth was slightly open, baring long, thin, cruel teeth. Its golden eyes never left the figure of Uncle Charlie walking towards it.

Peter found he couldn't move. He couldn't cry out. He couldn't look away. Uncle Charlie marched on.

Then, suddenly, he lifted his head as if he had scented something. He stopped. As the leopard sprang, the man instinctively flung up his arms as if to shield his face.

He fell on his back, and the beast stood over

him. One massive paw pressed on his chest, and the leopard sank down, half-covering Uncle Charlie's body. Its great jaws gripped the old man's neck, and slowly squeezed. It was soon over.

The leopard released its grip. It stood up, and looked straight at the boy. One foot still rested on the man's chest, like a triumphant game-hunter. Then it raised its chin and gave a short, snarling roar of victory. In a second it had gone. It simply disappeared, evaporated into the rush of darkness that wrapped itself round Peter.

It was a little while before Peter's parents found the two bodies, the old man dead, the boy unconscious. Later, Peter tried to talk to the anxious faces bending over him, but they shushed him gently and told him not to worry.

The doctor said Uncle Charlie had died of heart failure: there were no other signs of the cause of death. Peter could have his old room back, cleaned and cleared of all the African souvenirs.

"Gruesome things," his mother called them, as she gathered them up. She thought some of them might fetch a bit of money, especially that fur rug. But when she looked for it, she couldn't find it anywhere.

No one ever did find the leopard-skin rug. It had simply disappeared.